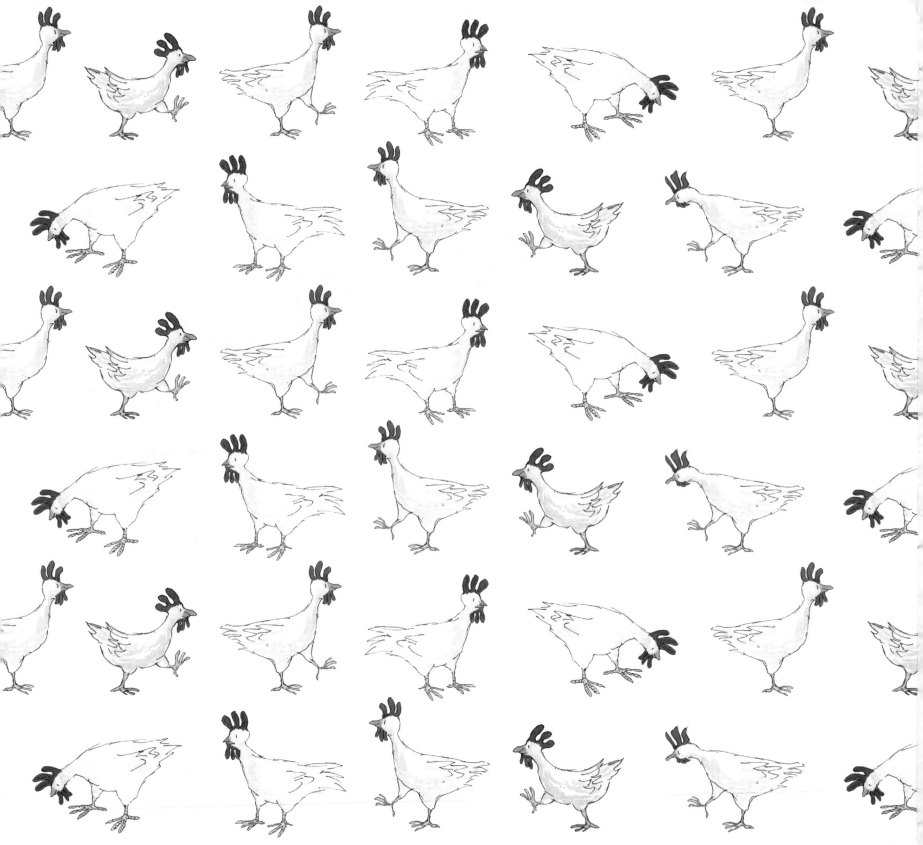

# A HEBRIDEAN ALPHABET

## BY DEBI GLIORI

Are you awake? All around is air.
You can't see it, but the Hebrides made it
just for us, just for this day.

Breathe it in . . .
then get your boots on.
Breakfast? Where first: shingly
beach or boggy burn?

Come on! Mind the cows.
Cross the cotton grass, past the old croft.

There's so much to do in a day.
Slide down the dunes, dam the burn.
Dig for treasure . . .

NO! Down, dog, get down!
She likes exploring everything.

Up here, you sometimes see eagles, circling over the empty village.

And far out at sea, there's the ferry, tracing a lacy wake in the blue, and further out, the fishing fleet, followed by gannets.

Talking of gannets, I'm hungry . . .
From here, up high, we can see the haar coming in,

wrapping round the headland,
inching across the island.
I'm not going in.
There are too many jellyfish.
JINGS!

Kayaks! Look! Out on the kyle. Loads of them.
And one for us,
beside the lobster creels on the machair.
Let's hope the mackerel are biting
as much as the midges.

No? Nothing?
Not even a single nibble?

Ochhh!
That
explains it.

The otter,
out there.

It's catching our fish.

Perfect. It's so quiet.
If you listen, you can
hear the rain.

If you *really* listen, you can hear
the distant sound of sheep.

But if you listen with your heart,
you'll hear the sound of the sun
slowly slipping into the sea.

Tide's coming back in.
We're all tired. Time to take the high road
home for tea.

Trudging uphill under an ultramarine sky.

Very tired.
Below us, the view is lit by the very last shaving
of a waning moon.

Wellies off, and into the warmth.

What a wonderful day!
Where did we put
the treasure?

X marks the spot.

XXXs on the window-pane.
(We love this place.)

You're yawning!
So are you!
You yawn like a cat.
Well, you yawn like a sheep.
I'm yawning like a
HUGE cave.
YAAaaaWWWwwwn.
Do it all again tomorrow?
YES!

To Marion and Kerr with thanks,
and for Lindsey with much love, as always

First published in 2016 by
BC Books, an imprint of Birlinn Limited
West Newington House, 10 Newington Road
Edinburgh EH9 1QS

www.bcbooksforkids.co.uk

ISBN: 978 1 78027 358 7

British Library Cataloguing-in-Publication Data
A catalogue record for this book is available from the British Library

Book design by Debi Gliori and James Hutcheson

Typeset in Yana Regular

Printed and bound by Livonia Print, Latvia